·A· FRUIT & VEGETABLE MAN

by **Roni Schotter**
Pictures by **Jeanette Winter**

Little, Brown and Company
Boston   Toronto   London

*To Melanie Kroupa and Susan Cohen for their loving care
and to Richard for (can it be?) twenty-five years of his*
— R. S.

Text copyright © 1993 by Roni Schotter
Illustrations copyright © 1993 by Jeanette Winter

First Edition

Library of Congress Cataloging-in-Publication Data

Schotter, Roni.
    A fruit and vegetable man / by Roni Schotter ; pictures by
Jeanette Winter. — 1st ed.
        p.   cm.
    Summary: Sun Ho first watches the artistic fruit and vegetable
man, Ruby Rubenstein, at work; then he begins helping in the store —
even offering something new: bean sprouts.
    ISBN 0-316-77467-7
    [1. Produce trade — Fiction.]   I. Winter, Jeanette, ill.
II. Title.
PZ7.S3765Fr   1993
[E] — dc20   92-17555

10 9 8 7 6 5 4 3 2 1

BER
Published simultaneously in Canada
by Little, Brown & Company (Canada) Limited

Printed in the United States of America

The paintings in this book were done in
acrylics on Strathmore Bristol paper.

Ruby Rubenstein was a fruit and vegetable man. His motto was "I take care." Six mornings a week, long before the sun was up, Ruby was.

"*Is it time,* Ruby?" his wife Trudy always asked from deep under the covers.

"It's time," Ruby always answered. Then he'd jump out of bed, touch his knees, then his toes, and hurry uptown to market to choose the ripest fruit and vegetables for his store.

For nearly fifty years it had been so — ever since he and Trudy first sailed across the ocean to make a new life together.

Every morning before school, Sun Ho and his sister, Young Mee, who with their family, had just flown across the sky to make a new life together, came to watch Ruby work his magic.

"Yo-ho, Mr. Ruby!" Sun Ho would call out. "Show me!"

And nodding to Sun Ho, Ruby would pile apples, tangerines, and pears in perfect pyramids, arrange grapes in diamonds, insert a head of lettuce as accent, then tuck in a bunch of broccoli or a bit of watercress for trim.

It was like seeing a great artist at work. Sun Ho felt honored to be there. "Like a painting, Mr. Ruby!" he would say shyly.

Ruby always smiled, and his smile filled Sun Ho with happiness and, deep inside, a strange feeling that was like wishing. Sun Ho watched as Ruby juggled cantaloupes, then cut them into wedges and packed them neatly in plastic. Inside Sun Ho, the feeling that was like wishing grew stronger.

"He's an artist, all right," Old Ella from up the
block always said, pocketing an apple and a handful
of prunes.

Ruby didn't mind. He'd just wink and utter one
wonderful word: "Taste!" Then he'd offer whatever
he had on special that day to Sun Ho, his sister, and
anyone who wanted.

"What would we *do* without Ruby?" Mary
Morrissey asked the crowd one gray afternoon. The
people of Delano Street sighed and shook their heads
at such a terrible thought.

"Mr. Ruby," Sun Ho said, "he's one of a kind."

   Yes, everyone on Delano Street appreciated Ruby.
But Ruby was getting old. Lately, when he got up to
touch his knees and his toes, there was a stiffness
Ruby pretended he didn't feel and a creaking Trudy
pretended she didn't hear. And sometimes, though
Ruby never would admit it, there was a wish that he
could stay a little longer in bed with Trudy.

"Ruby," Trudy said to him one morning from under the covers. "Long ago you and I made a promise. We said if ever we got old, we'd sell the business and go to live in the mountains. *Is it time, Ruby?*"

"NO!!" Ruby thundered. And he leapt out of bed, did *twice* his usual number of exercises, and ran off to market.

As if to prove he was as young as ever, he worked especially hard at the store that day and made some of his most beautiful designs.

That afternoon, Sun Ho came by as Ruby was arranging potatoes in his own special way. Sun Ho watched as Ruby whirled them in the air and tossed them with such skill that they landed perfectly, one next to the other in a neat row.

"Yo-ho, Mr. Ruby!" Sun Ho said, filled with admiration. "Teach me?"

Proudly, Ruby grabbed an Idaho and two russets and taught Sun Ho how to juggle. Next he taught him how to pile grapefruits to keep them from falling. By the time Sun Ho's parents stopped by, Ruby had even taught Sun Ho how to work the register. Then he sat Sun Ho down and told him how, early every morning, he went to market to choose his fruit and vegetables.

"Take me!" Sun Ho pleaded, the feeling that was like wishing so big now he felt he might burst. "Please?"

Ruby thought for only a moment. Then he spoke. "My pleasure," he announced.

So early the next day, while Venus still sparkled in
the dark morning sky, Ruby took Sun Ho to market.
Sun Ho had an excellent nose, and together he and

Ruby sniffed out the most fragrant fruit and sampled
the choicest chicory. Then Ruby showed Sun Ho
how he talked and teased and argued his way to the
best prices.

All the rest of that long day, Sun Ho felt special. And Ruby? He felt, well . . . tired. Whenever Trudy was busy with a customer, Ruby leaned over and pretended to tie his shoe, but what he did, really, was *yawn*. By afternoon, Ruby was running out of the store every few minutes. "The fruit!" he'd yell to Trudy. "Got to fix the fruit!" he'd say, but once outside, what he did, really, was *sneeze*.

"To your health, Mr. Ruby," Sun Ho whispered, sneaking him a handkerchief.

"Thank you, Mr. Sun Ho," Ruby said, quietly blowing his nose.

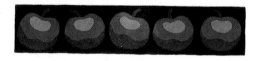

That evening it began to snow on Delano Street.
It snowed all night, and by morning the street was cold
and white, the color of fresh cauliflower.

For the first time in many years, Ruby woke up
feeling sick. His face was red, his forehead hot. "No
work today," Trudy said. "Ruby's Fruit and Vegetable
is closed until further notice." What would the people
of Delano Street do without him? Ruby wondered.
But he was too sick to care.

When Sun Ho arrived at the store that day and saw
that it was closed, he was worried. Where was Ruby?

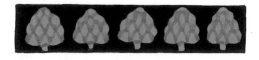

Upstairs in his bed, Ruby dozed, dreaming of spring
and fresh apricots. Once, when he opened his eyes,
Sun Ho was standing next to him . . . or was he?

"No worries," Sun Ho seemed to say. "I take care."
Then as strangely as he had appeared, Sun Ho
disappeared. Was Ruby dreaming?

For the next three days, for the first time in his life, Ruby was too sick to think or worry about his store. He stayed deep under the covers, enjoying Trudy's loving care, and more than that, her barley soup. On the morning of the fourth day, he felt well enough to worry. On the morning of the fifth day, a Saturday, there was no stopping him. "My store!" he shouted. Leaning on Trudy's arm, he put on his clothes. Then he rushed off to reopen.

What a surprise when he arrived! The store was open. In fact, it looked as if it had never been shut. The peppers were in pyramids, the dates in diamonds, the winter tomatoes in triangles. Sun Ho's father was helping Old Ella to a pound of carrots. Sun Ho's mother was at the register. Young Mee was polishing pears. And, in the center of it all, Sun Ho stood smiling, offering customers a taste of something new — bean sprouts!

When they saw Ruby, everyone cheered. Ruby
bowed with pleasure.

"I took care, Mr. Ruby!" Sun Ho called out proudly.

"I see," Ruby answered. "You're a fruit and
vegetable man, Sun Ho, like me."

Sun Ho's face turned the color of Ruby's radishes.
The feeling that was like wishing was gone now. In its
place was a different feeling: pride.

"*Is it time,* Ruby?" Trudy whispered.

Ruby sighed. He thought about how much he liked
Sun Ho and his family and how carefully they had kept
his store. He thought about the stiffness and creaking
in his knees. He thought about the mountains and
about Trudy's loving care. More than that, he thought
about her barley soup.

"It's time," he said finally.

Now Sun Ho is a fruit and vegetable man! Every morning, long before the sun is up, long before it's time for school, Sun Ho and his family are up, ready to hurry to market to choose the ripest fruit and vegetables for their store.

And Ruby? He's still a fruit and vegetable man . . .
only now he and Trudy grow their own.